This
MOUSE WORKS

Classics Collection Storybook

belongs to

_____

DISNEY's
Cinderella
CLASSIC STORYBOOK

MOUSE WORKS

Find us at **www.disneybooks.com** *for more Mouse Works fun!*

© 1988, 1993, 1998 Disney Enterprises, Inc.
Adapted by Michael Paxton
Illustrated by Atelier Philippe Harchy
Printed in the United States of America
ISBN: 1-57082-797-4
1 3 5 7 9 10 8 6 4 2

CSRVCIN97-13

Once upon a time in a small kingdom there lived a
beautiful girl named Cinderella. She and her widowed
father led a peaceful, rich life. Her father was a kind
and devoted gentleman, and Cinderella loved him
dearly. But he knew that Cinderella needed a mother,
so he remarried. Cinderella's stepmother had two
daughters of her own, Drizella and Anastasia.

Soon, however, Cinderella's father died, leaving Cinderella in her stepmother's care. Cinderella soon realized her new family was jealous of her charm and beauty. Her stepmother grew more coldhearted every day. She cared only for her own daughters.

Before long Cinderella was forced to become a servant in her own home. She waited on her grim stepmother and vain stepsisters hand and foot.

But through it all, Cinderella still believed her dreams would come true someday.

In her attic bedroom, she was awakened each day by the little birds' sweet songs.

"Yes, I know it's a lovely morning," she sighed. "But I had such a lovely dream..."

The birds and the mice of the house wanted to hear about her dream. But Cinderella wouldn't tell them. "If you tell, it won't come true," she said.

Her stepsisters rang for breakfast. It was time to go to work.

"Well, there's one thing," Cinderella said brightly to her friends. "They can't order me to stop dreaming!"

Suddenly Jaq, the little mouse, came running in. A visitor had been caught in a trap! "Hurry, Cinderelly! Come-come!"

Cinderella was concerned because she really cared for the mice. She always made sure they had enough to eat, and even made little clothes for them to wear. She dashed out of her room and ran down the long stairway.

11

When Cinderella reached the trap, she found
a plump little fellow caught inside. He was
very frightened at first, but she and Jaq soon
convinced him they were his friends.
Cinderella gave him a little shirt, cap, and
shoes, and the name "Octavius." Then she
decided to call him "Gus" for short.

Knowing the other mice would take care of Gus, Cinderella headed for the kitchen to start breakfast. "Don't forget to warn Gus about Lucifer!" she called out to Jaq.

Jaq explained to Gus that Lucifer the cat belonged to Cinderella's stepmother, and he was not very nice at all!

In the kitchen, Cinderella gently called to Bruno the dog. "Dreaming again?" she asked. Bruno nodded excitedly. "Chasing Lucifer, I bet! Well, you better get rid of those dreams if you want to keep a nice warm bed." When Cinderella couldn't convince Bruno that even Lucifer might have a good side, she took him out into the yard.

"It's breakfast time, everybody!" Cinderella called sweetly. The chickens gathered around Cinderella as she tossed them their food. Major the horse watched them happily from the barn. The mice were invited, too, but first they had to get out of the house—past mean old Lucifer.

19

Jaq tiptoed quietly up beside the nasty cat, who was drinking a big bowl of fresh milk. With one swift kick, Jaq knocked the cat's paw out from under him and...splat! Lucifer's face fell right into the bowl. Now the mice had time to scurry past Lucifer and out into the yard.

"Oh, there you are! I was wondering where you were!" Cinderella smiled. She tossed some kernels of corn to the mice. Gus's eyes were too big for his stomach, and he gathered more corn than he could carry.

Paying attention only to his food, Gus ran smack into Lucifer, who wanted to eat him for breakfast! But Gus was so loaded down with corn, he couldn't get away. Thinking fast, Jaq knocked a broom over on Lucifer to help Gus escape.

With Lucifer in pursuit, Gus ran up onto the kitchen table and hid under a teacup. Lucifer began to lift the cup where Gus was hiding, when...

Ring! Ring! Cinderella's stepmother and stepsisters were impatient for breakfast.

"Cinderella! Cinderella!" Their shrill voices echoed through the house and out into the yard. Cinderella rushed into the kitchen and chased Lucifer from the table before he could grab poor Gus. Then she began to prepare the breakfast trays for the family. She was in such a hurry, she didn't notice that Gus was still hiding under one of the teacups.

Carefully balancing the trays, Cinderella climbed the long stairway to the bedrooms. But as she reached the top of the staircase, she heard a familiar screech.

"Cinderella!" It was Drizella.

Cinderella rushed into Drizella's bedroom. "Take that ironing and have it ready in an hour!" Drizella demanded.

Next Cinderella went to Anastasia's room to drop off her breakfast. "It's about time!" Anastasia whined.

Just as Cinderella left the last tray with her stepmother, she heard a frantic scream. Anastasia had discovered Gus under her teacup! She ran to her mother to tattle.

"Come here!" Cinderella's stepmother ordered from the dark shadows of her bed.

Cinderella moved toward the bed and pleaded, "Oh, please, you don't think that I—"

"Hold your tongue!" her stepmother commanded. Assuming Cinderella was guilty, her stepmother gave her a list of extra chores to do—including giving Lucifer a bath!

Meanwhile, at the royal palace, the widowed king had his own problems. His son, the Prince, was drifting farther away from him. "I'm lonely in this desolate old palace," he complained to the Grand Duke. "I want to hear the pitter-patter of little feet again." The King decided to arrange a ball in the Prince's honor. If they invited every eligible maiden in the land, surely the Prince would choose one to marry.

Later that morning a messenger
knocked on Cinderella's door.
"Open in the name of the King!"
he cried.

Cinderella answered the
door and was handed an urgent
letter from the palace. The
messenger's bag was filled
with invitations.

Cinderella's stepmother grabbed the letter and read it out loud. When they learned that there was to be a ball in the Prince's honor and all eligible young women were invited, Drizella and Anastasia could hardly contain their excitement.

Realizing that she, too, was invited, Cinderella quickly joined in.

Her stepsisters laughed at the idea of Cinderella's going to the ball.

But her stepmother said, "I see no reason you can't go...if you get all your work done and find something suitable to wear..."

Cinderella searched for the right gown to wear. She decided on one that had belonged to her mother. When the mice commented that it looked a little old-fashioned, Cinderella smiled. She knew that with some help and a little work, it would be a wonderful new dress.

"Cinderella! Cinderella!" her stepsisters and stepmother called out frantically.

"Oh, now what do they want?" Cinderella sighed.

Now that Cinderella had to attend to her stepmother and stepsisters, she knew that her dress would have to wait. But after she left, the mice felt sorry for their Cinderelly. They knew that she would never get her dress done in time for the ball.

Her friends all decided to pitch in.
Gus and Jaq found a pretty pink sash
and a shiny string of blue beads that
Cinderella's frivolous stepsisters had
thrown away. Soon, with a needle and
thread, the simple dress was turned
into a beautiful gown.

Evening fell over the kingdom and it was time for the ball. Coach after coach pulled up to the royal palace. Eligible maidens were already lining up to meet the handsome prince.

Alas, it was too late for Cinderella. Her
stepmother and stepsisters had kept her busy
right up until it was time to leave for the ball.
Now she could only dream about what it
would be like to meet the Prince.

Then Cinderella heard something behind her. She turned and saw the birds and the mice opening her closet to reveal her new dress. Overwhelmed, she thanked her little friends for all their hard work. Now, if she hurried, maybe she could still make it to the ball.

Cinderella dressed quickly and ran down the stairs to join her stepsisters.

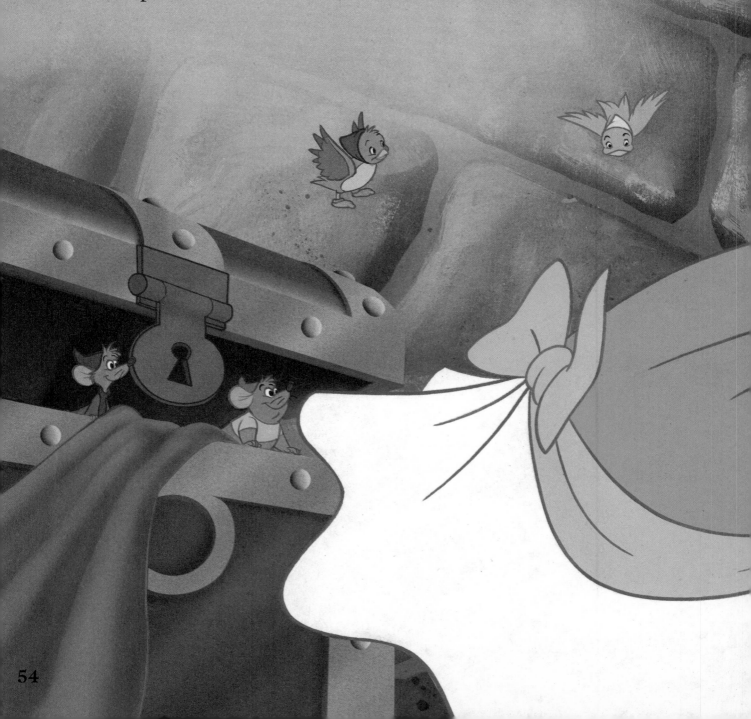

Unfortunately, when Drizella and Anastasia saw Cinderella's new dress, they also noticed their discarded beads and sash. Furious, the stepsisters tore them off the dress, ruining it for good. Cinderella's stepmother simply stood by and watched, satisfied that Cinderella would not be going to the ball.

Heartbroken, Cinderella ran to the garden in tears. Now her dream would never come true. She cried softly, hopelessly. "There's nothing left to believe in...nothing..." she sobbed. Bruno and Major watched helplessly. Poor Cinderella!

Then a strange glow appeared in the garden.

Light seemed to gather around Cinderella. Soon a kindly old woman appeared. It was Cinderella's fairy godmother! She told Cinderella to dry her tears. Knowing that Cinderella had really not given up hope and still believed in her dreams, the fairy godmother promised that she, too, would go to the ball.

With a wave of her wand and some magical words, the fairy godmother turned a garden pumpkin into a beautiful coach. Cinderella and the animals couldn't believe their eyes!

Then, before they knew it, Gus, Jaq, and two of their friends were turned into four proud white horses. Major became the coachman, and Bruno was transformed into the footman.

63

But the fairy godmother was not finished. She still had to change Cinderella's rags into an elegant gown!

"Just leave it to me. What a gown this will be!" she told Cinderella with confidence. She waved her wand with gusto and dressed Cinderella in a splendid new gown and sparkling glass slippers.

Before Cinderella left for the palace, her fairy godmother warned her that the magic would not last forever. Cinderella had to be sure to return home by the stroke of midnight. That was when everything would change back to what it had been—a pumpkin, four mice, a horse, and a dog. Cinderella thanked her fairy godmother, and then she was off to the ball!

Cinderella arrived at the palace entrance just as the Prince was being introduced to Drizella and Anastasia. He looked up to see Cinderella enter the ballroom.

Immediately enchanted, he quickly brushed past Drizella and Anastasia to greet her. Cinderella was captivated by the handsome man who bowed graciously before her.

Meanwhile, happy that the Prince had finally shown an interest in someone, the King ordered the orchestra to play a waltz.

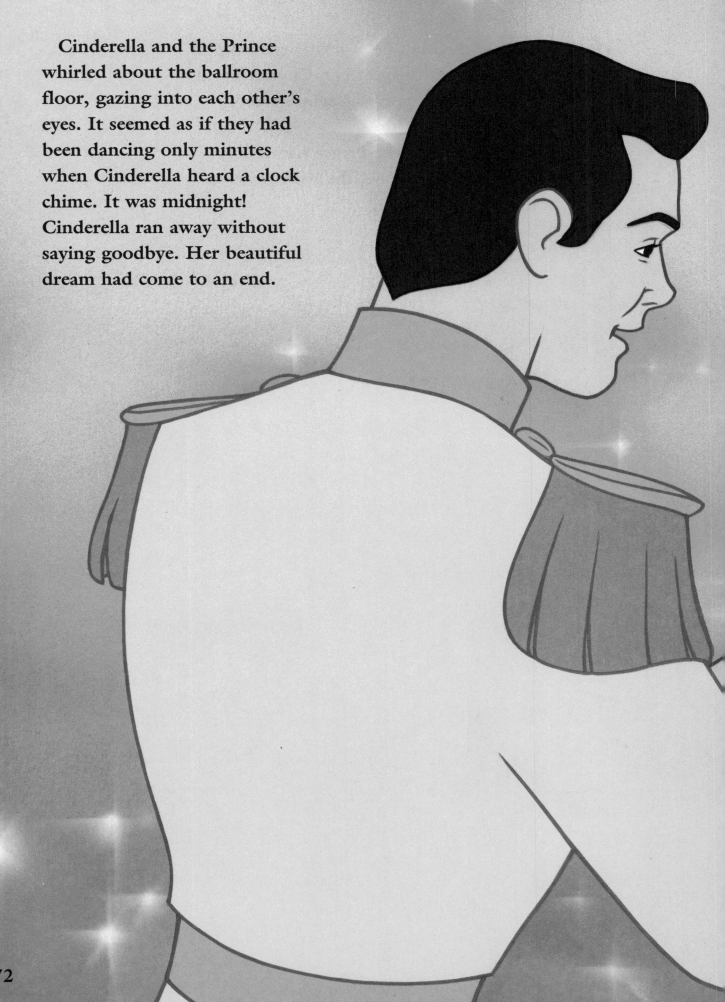

Cinderella and the Prince whirled about the ballroom floor, gazing into each other's eyes. It seemed as if they had been dancing only minutes when Cinderella heard a clock chime. It was midnight! Cinderella ran away without saying goodbye. Her beautiful dream had come to an end.

She raced through the ballroom and down the
long palace stairway. She ran so fast that neither the
Prince nor the Grand Duke could catch her, but she
lost one of her glass slippers along the way.

Cinderella jumped into the coach just as the Grand
Duke found her slipper and called for the guards.
"Follow that coach!" he yelled frantically.

The guards chased Cinderella's coach, but never found her. The magic had worn off.

"Oh, it was wonderful!" Cinderella sighed. Then she noticed she still had a glass slipper. She looked up into the sky with a smile. Hoping her fairy godmother could hear, she whispered, "Thank you for everything!"

The next day, news spread that the Prince was searching for the mysterious young woman who had lost her glass slipper. He was madly in love with her. So by royal decree, the girl whose foot fit the glass slipper would marry the Prince. And Cinderella's stepmother was determined that either Drizella or Anastasia would be the Prince's bride.

Cinderella was overwhelmed by the news. She walked to her room in a daze, dreamily humming a waltz she had heard at the ball. Observing her, Cinderella's stepmother realized that Cinderella was the Prince's mysterious love.

Gus and Jaq tried to warn Cinderella, but her hateful stepmother locked her in her room just as the Grand Duke arrived.

Gus and Jaq peeked under the door and watched the evil stepmother hide the key in her pocket. "We just gotta get that key!" Jaq cried.

"May I present my daughters, Drizella and Anastasia," Cinderella's stepmother said to the Grand Duke. She offered him some tea, but he wanted to try the glass slipper on her daughters and be on his way.

While his footman tried the glass slipper on Anastasia's foot, Jaq crawled into the stepmother's pocket and stole the key. He and Gus struggled up the long stairway to Cinderella's room and slid the key under her door.

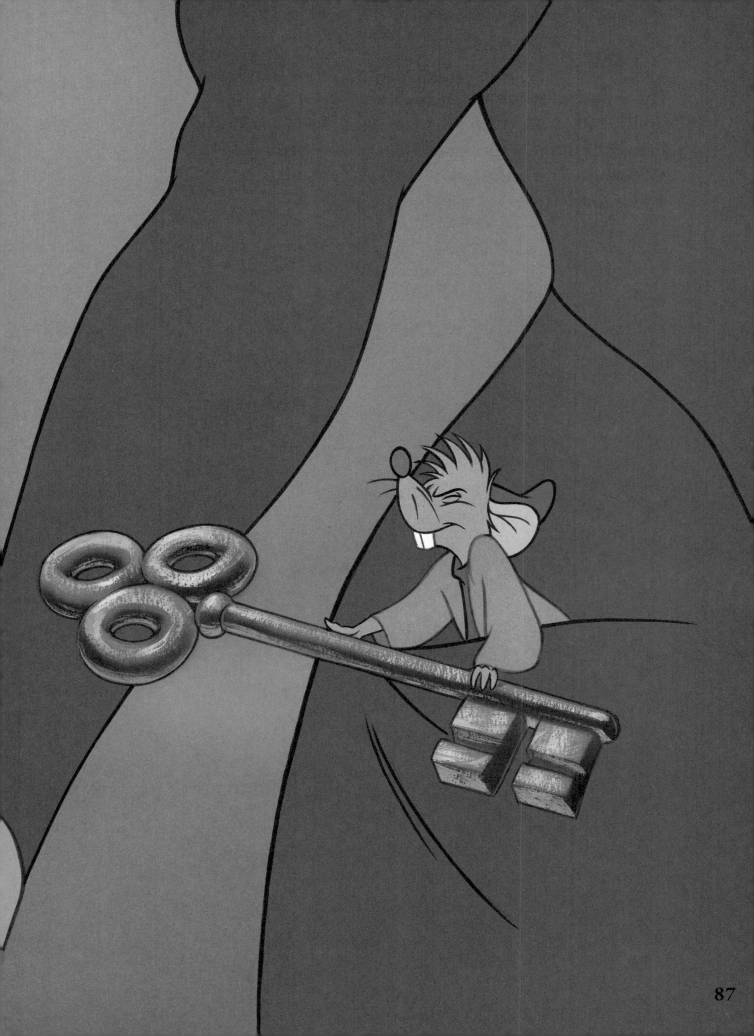

The footman tried one last time to fit the slipper on Drizella. "I'll make it fit!" she screeched. She pushed and squeezed, but the slipper would not go on her foot.

"If there are no other ladies in the household, we will bid you good day!" said the Grand Duke.

Just then, Cinderella called out from the top of the stairs. "Your Grace! Your Grace! Please wait!" Everyone gasped as Cinderella rushed down the stairway to the Grand Duke.

Cinderella's stepmother demanded that Cinderella not be allowed to try on the glass slipper. The Grand Duke ignored her, but as the footman approached Cinderella, her stepmother tripped him with her cane. The slipper flew into the air and shattered on the floor.

But Cinderella reached into her pocket and presented the other glass slipper. Relieved, the Grand Duke took the slipper and placed it on her foot. It was a perfect fit!

Soon the bells of the palace rang out on
Cinderella's wedding day. The King and the
Grand Duke smiled as they watched the
happy couple get married.

But no one was happier than Cinderella.
At last her dreams had all come true.

Disney's Classic Storybook COLLECTION ™

Relive the movies one book at a time.

ALADDIN
ALICE IN WONDERLAND
THE ARISTOCATS
BAMBI
BEAUTY AND THE BEAST

THE BLACK CAULDRON
CINDERELLA
DUMBO
THE FOX AND THE HOUND
THE GREAT MOUSE DETECTIVE

HERCULES
THE HUNCHBACK OF NOTRE DAME
THE JUNGLE BOOK
LADY AND THE TRAMP
THE LION KING

THE LITTLE MERMAID
MICKEY'S CHRISTMAS CAROL
OLIVER & COMPANY
ONE HUNDRED AND ONE DALMATIAN
PETER PAN

PINOCCHIO
POCAHONTAS
THE RESCUERS
THE RESCUERS DOWN UNDER
ROBIN HOOD

SLEEPING BEAUTY
SNOW WHITE AND THE SEVEN DWARF
THE SWORD IN THE STONE
TOY STORY
WINNIE THE POOH

FILM MANIFESTOS AND GLOBAL CINEMA CULTURES